THIS WALKER BOOK BELONGS TO:

For Devadasi

·First published 1988 by
Walker Books Ltd
87 Vauxhall Wallk
London SE11 5HJ

© 1988 Jez Alborough

This edition published 1990

4 6 8 10 9 7 5 3

Printed in Hong Kong

British Library Cataloguing in Publication Data
A catalogue record for this book is
available from the British Library.

ISBN 0-7445-1493-2

ESTHER'S TRUNK

poot!

AN ELEPHANTASY BY

Jez Alborough

WALKER BOOKS
AND SUBSIDIARIES
LONDON · BOSTON · SYDNEY

Esther felt a proper chump.

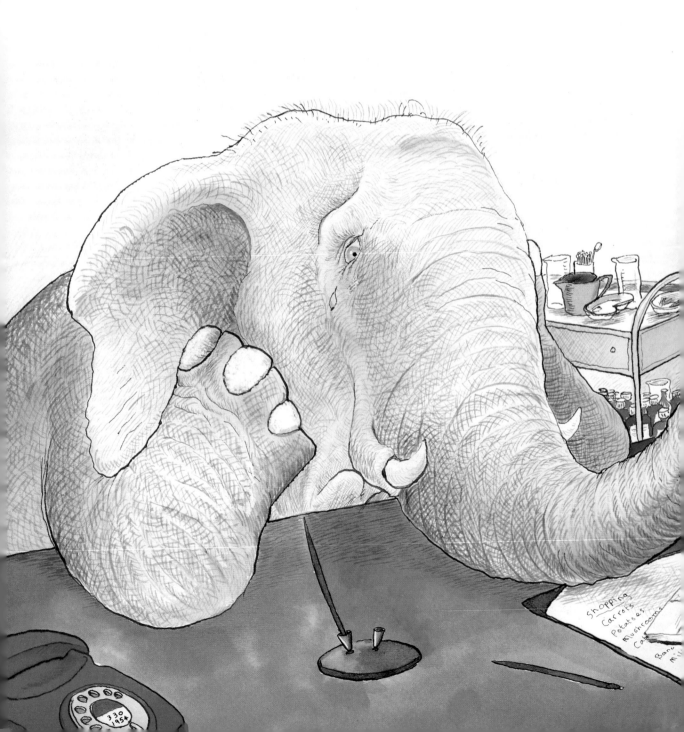

"My trunk," she sobbed,
"has lost its trump!"

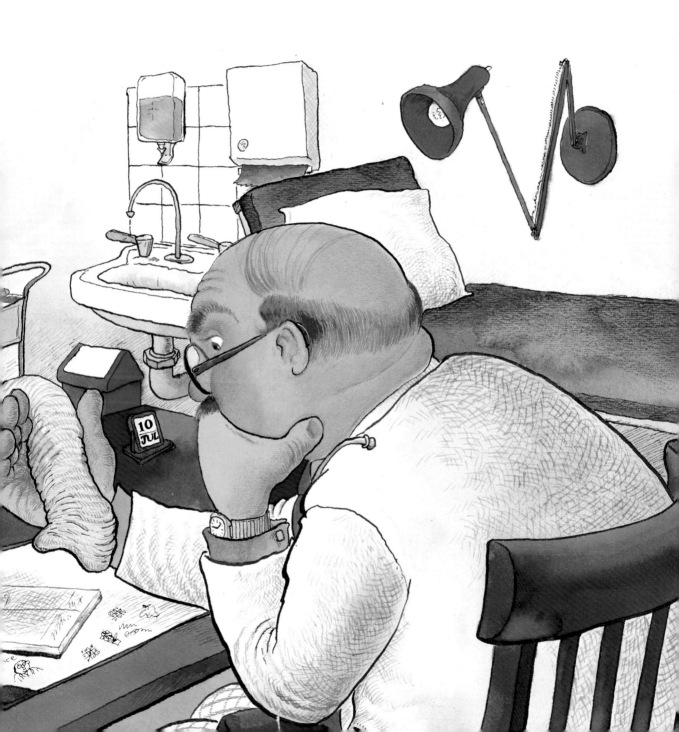

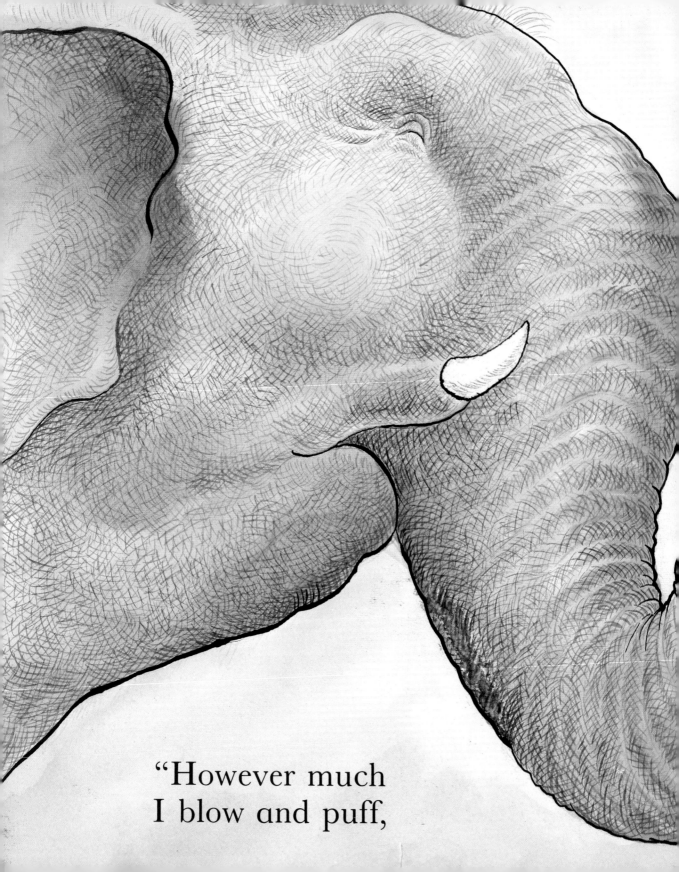

"However much
I blow and puff,

it never seems
to be enough."

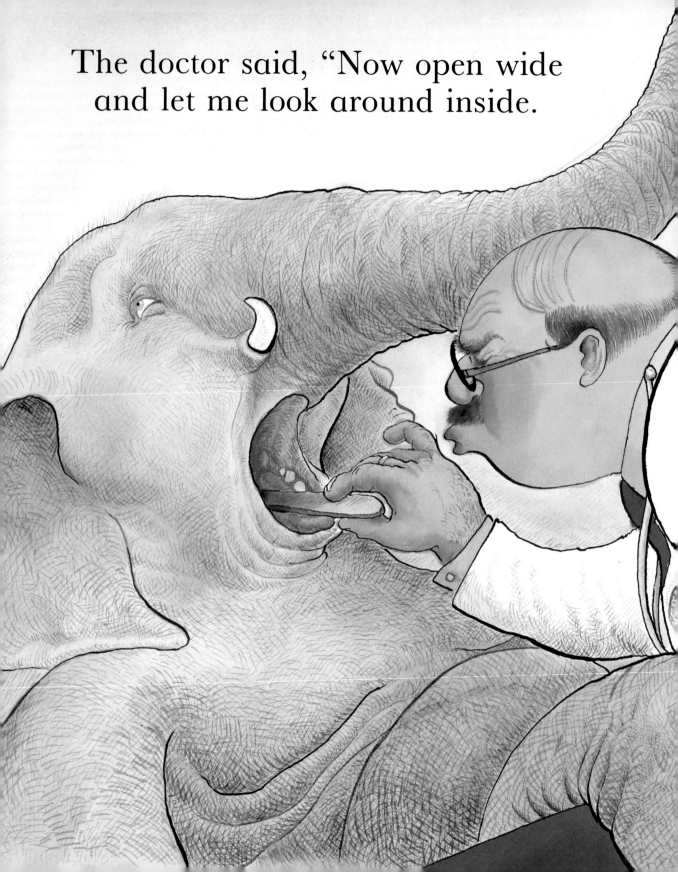

The doctor said, "Now open wide
and let me look around inside.

Your throat is fine ...
your tongue seems well ...
but pooh! what is that awful smell?"

"I think I'll try another test.
Just let me listen to your chest.

Both your lungs are clear and strong,
but my oh my, what *is* that pong?"

Now the doctor has a hunch.
He asks what Esther ate for lunch.

When she answers, "Cheese and pickle,"
he knows the cure ...

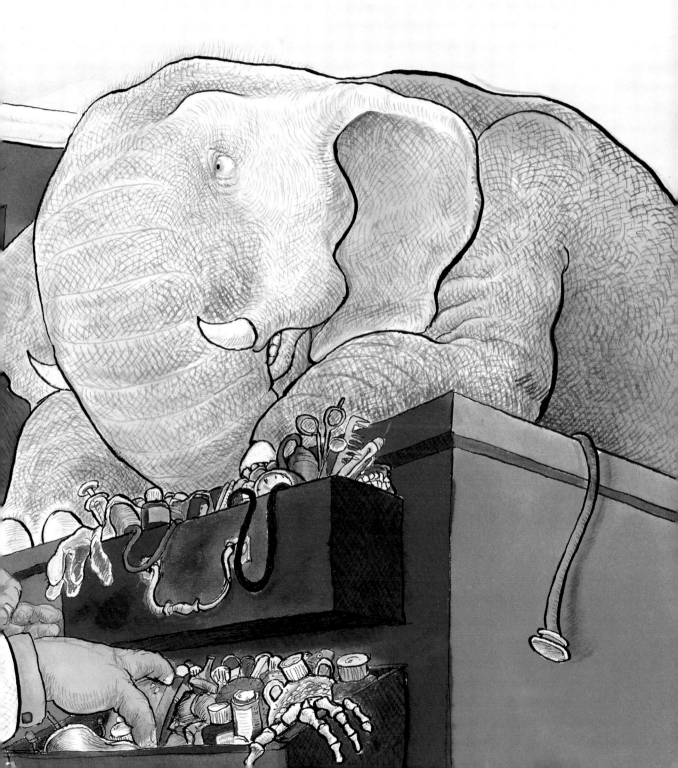

a feather's tickle!

"A ... ha ..." said Esther, "stop it, *please!*
Be careful or you'll make me sneeze."

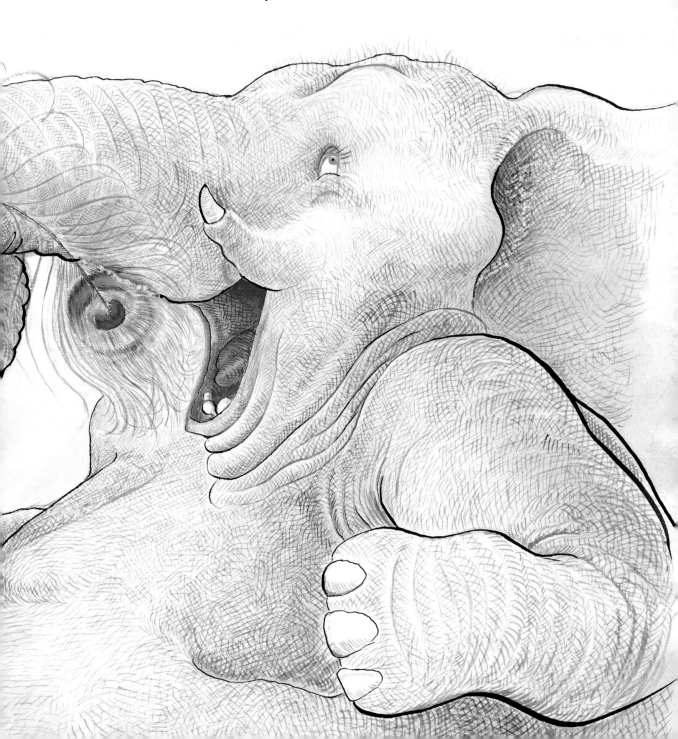

"A ... ha ... a ... ha ... a ... stop it, do ...

aha … aha … aha … aaaaa …"

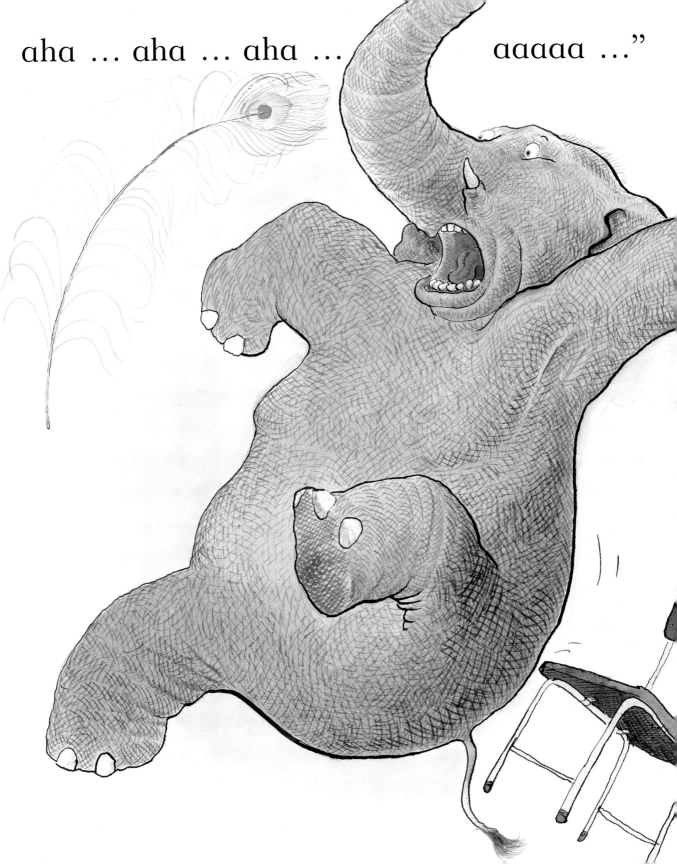

"CHOOOOOO!"

"That's what I smelt!" the doctor cried.

"A pickled gherkin stuck inside!"

"Now try and blow
without that lump."

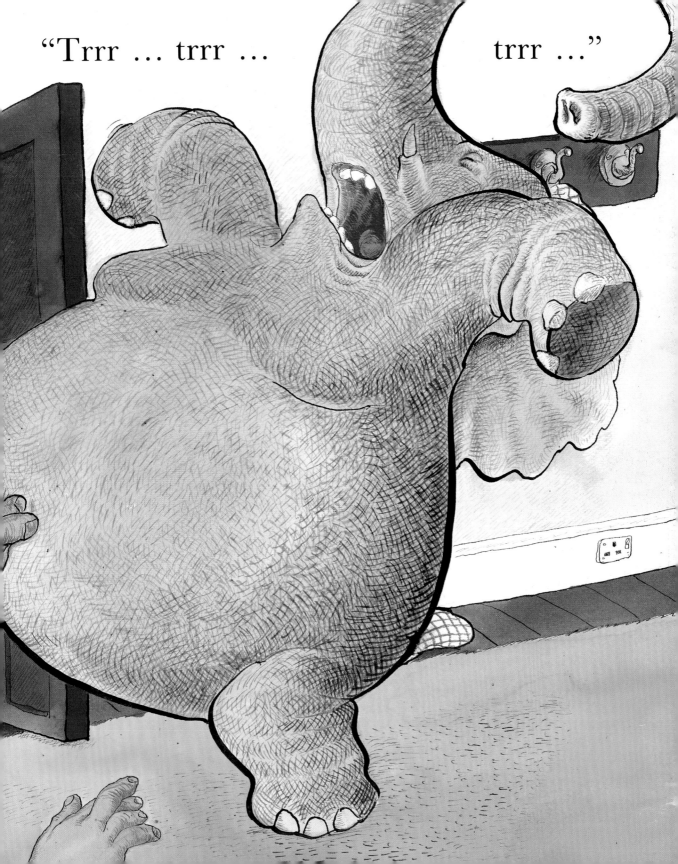

"TRRRUMP!"

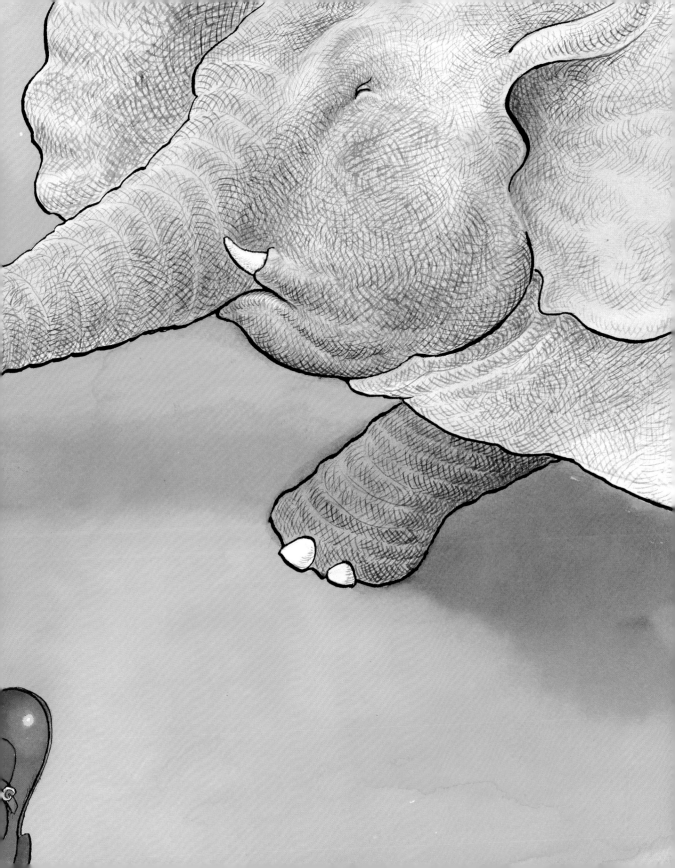

The doctor said, "You see, my dear,
the treatment now is very clear.

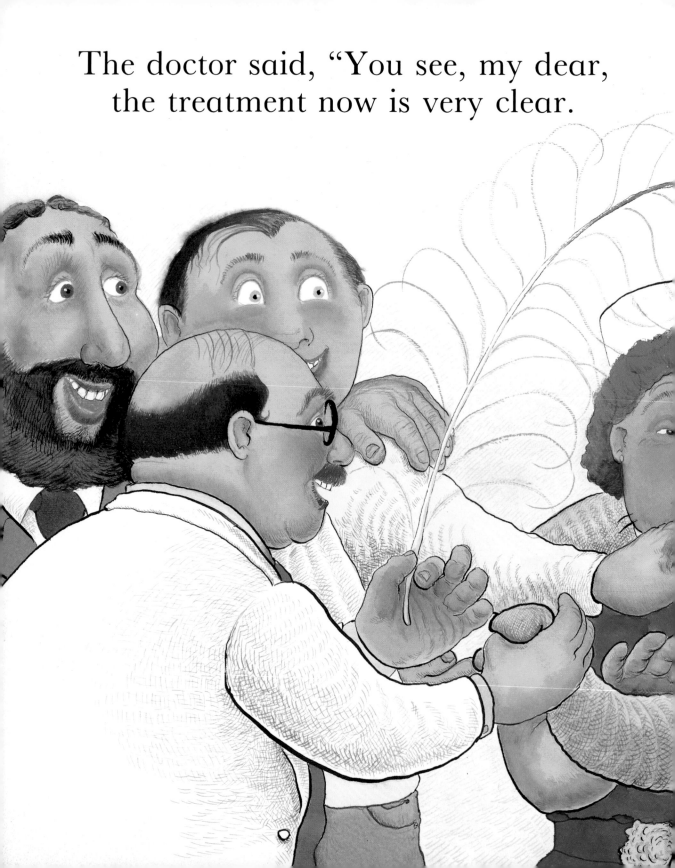

Next time you get in such a pickle,
here's the feather ...
try a tickle!"

MORE WALKER PAPERBACKS
For You to Enjoy
Also by Jez Alborough

BEAKY

Beaky has a bright blue beak, furry flaps and a curly orange tail.
But what is he?
That's what he tries to find out in this touching, intriguing
and irresistible tale for young children.

Lots of ecological detail accompanies the story."
The Times Educational Supplement
ISBN 0-7445-1789-3   £3.99

CUPBOARD BEAR

Lazy bear just loves to dream
Of his favourite thing – ICE CREAM!
But bear's sweet dream turns to sour nightmare,
When he finds one day his cupboard's bare!

ISBN 0-7445-1731-1   £3.99

WHERE'S MY TEDDY?

A small boy and a gigantic bear have a
momentous encounter in the woods!

"A very appealing story … will bear endless repetition."
Patricia Hodge, The Mail on Sunday

ISBN 0-7445-3058-X   £3.99

Walker Paperbacks are available from most booksellers, or by post from B.B.C.S., P.O. Box 941, Hull, North Humberside HU1 3YQ

24 hour telephone credit card line 01482 224626

To order, send: Title, author, ISBN number and price for each book ordered, your full name and address,
cheque or postal order payable to BBCS for the total amount and allow the following for postage and packing:
UK and BFPO: £1.00 for the first book, and 50p for each additional book to a maximum of £3.50.
Overseas and Eire: £2.00 for the first book, £1.00 for the second and 50p for each additional book.

Prices and availability are subject to change without notice.